DATE DUE

DEC 1 ~ ~ | |||| 2 9 1000

A DINO **EASY** READER

Rex and Lilly

Family Time

Stories by Laurie Krasny Brown

Pictures by Marc Brown

Little, Brown and Company

Boston   New York   Toronto   London

*For all the champion teachers and readers
at Derby Academy*

First Edition
A Dino Easy Reader and the Dinosaur logo are trademarks of Little,
Brown and Company.
Library of Congress Cataloging-in-Publication Data
Brown, Laurene Krasny.
    Rex and Lilly family time / stories by Laurie Krasny Brown ;
pictures by Marc Brown. — 1st ed.
        p.   cm. — (A Dino easy reader)
    Contents: Happy birthday, Mom! — Robot Rob — The best pet.
    ISBN 0-316-11385-9 (lib. bdg.)
    [1. Dinosaurs — Fiction. 2. Brothers and sisters — Fiction.]
I. Brown, Marc Tolon, ill. II. Title. III. Series: Brown, Laurene Krasny.
Dino easy reader.
PZ7.B816114Re   1995
[E] — dc20   93-24162

10 9 8 7 6 5 4 3 2 1
WOR
Published simultaneously in Canada
by Little, Brown & Company (Canada) Limited

Printed in the United States of America

Contents

Happy Birthday, Mom!

"Surprise, surprise, surprise," said Rex.

"This will be Mom's best birthday!"

"Shh!" said Lilly. "Mom will hear you!"

"This will be the best frosting," said Lilly.

"Yellow!"

"Or blue. I like blue frosting," said Rex.

"Can I help?" asked Mom.

"Please, Mom!" said Rex.

"Don't help! Don't look!"

"What can I draw on Mom's card?"

asked Rex.

"Draw something Mom likes," said Lilly.

Rex tried to think. What does Mom like?

"Can I help?" asked Dad.

"Please, Dad!" said Lilly. "Don't help!

This is a surprise."

"Let's set the table," said Lilly.

"Forks here, spoons here."

"Hats here!" said Rex.

"Mom," said Rex and Lilly,

"you can come in now!"

"Surprise! Surprise! Happy Birthday, Mom!"

"Oh, my!" said Mom.

"This is my best birthday!

And you did *all* this with no help!"

"Oh, Mom," said Lilly,

"you can help us *now.*"

"I can?" said Mom.

"You can help us clean up!" said Rex.

Robot Rob

"We have too much to do," said Lilly.

"We need help!" said Rex.

"We need a housekeeper," said Mom.

"That will be my present," said Dad.

"A housekeeper!"

Knock, knock!

"Is that the housekeeper?" asked Dad.

"I'll see," said Rex.

"How do you do?" said Robot Rob.

"I am here to help!"

"Wow!" said Rex.

"Come in!" said Mom.

"I will wash for you,"

Robot Rob said to Mom.

"Thank you, Robot Rob!" said Mom.

Rob washed.

Rob washed some more.

Rob washed more and more and more.

"Stop, Rob!" said Mom.

"You have washed too much!"

"You can help us, Robot Rob!" said Lilly.

"You can help us pick up," said Rex.

Rob picked up.

Rob picked up some more.

Rob picked up more and more
and more.

"Stop, Rob!" said Rex and Lilly.

"You have picked up too much!"

"Can you help me?" asked Dad.

"Can you help me cut the grass?"

Rob cut.

Rob cut some more.

Rob cut more and more and more.

"Stop, Rob!" said Dad.

"You have cut too much!"

"Rob is too much help," said Lilly.

"We can clean the house," said Rex.

"Thank you for your help,"

Lilly said to Robot Rob.

"But you are much too much help!"

"Now that you do your own jobs,

you can have your own pets!" said Dad.

"Let's get them now!" said Rex and Lilly.

"Dad, may I have a dog?" asked Rex.

"A dog is the best pet!"

"No, Rex, not a dog," said Dad.

"A dog is too much trouble."

"Dad, may I have a cat?" asked Lilly.

"A cat is the best pet."

"No, Lilly, not a cat," said Dad.

"A cat is too much trouble."

"How about a bird?" asked Lilly.

"A bird can be the best pet!"

"No, not a bird either," said Dad.

"Too much trouble."

"No dog! No cat!" said Rex.

"Then what pet *can* we have?"

"Fish!" said Dad. "Fish are the best pets.

And they are not too much trouble."

"I like the yellow fish," said Lilly.

"I like the blue fish," said Rex.

Lilly put her fish in the tank.

Rex put his fish in, too.

The fish swam and swam.

"Is that all they do?" asked Rex.

A week later, Lilly said, "Look, Rex!

Look at all the fish!"

"Wow!" said Rex.

"Fish *are* the best pets!" said Rex.

"And we get more all the time!" said Lilly.